S0-AHK-639

DISCARDED

WAYNE PUBLIC LIBRARY

JUN 1 2 2012

What Shall We Eat?

Helen Lanz

SEA-TO-SEA

Mankato Collingwood London

This edition first published in 2012 by

Sea-to-Sea Publications
Distributed by Black Rabbit Books
P.O. Box 3263, Mankato, Minnesota 56002

Copyright © Sea-to-Sea Publications 2012

Printed in China

All rights reserved.

9 8 7 6 5 4 3 2

Published by arrangement with the Watts
Publishing Group Ltd, London.

Library of Congress Cataloging-in-Publication Data

Lanz, Helen.
 What shall we eat? / by Helen Lanz.
    p. cm. -- (Go green)
 Includes index.
 ISBN 978-1-59771-305-4 (library binding)
 1. Food industry and trade--Juvenile literature. 2. Food--Juvenile literature.
I. Title.
 HD9000.5.L325 2012
 338.1'9--dc22
                                    2011004379

Series Editor: Julia Bird
Design: D.R. ink
Artworks: Mike Phillips

Picture credits: Ralf Antblad/istockphoto: 9t: Paul Barton/Corbis:
front cover t; Mark Boulton/Alamy: 25cr; Brazil Photos/Alamy: 18t;
Alan Crawford/istockphoto: 1, 13t; Digital Vision/Getty Images: 8;
Esemelwe/istockphoto: 11b: Fotocraft/Alamy: 26; Simon
Hadley/Alamy: 21; Helicefoto/istockphoto: front cover cr; Dana
Hoff/Corbis: 17t; Imagebroker/Alamy: 25bl; Image Source Pink
/Alamy: 19b; Jaileybug/Alamy: 24; Linda Kennedy/Alamy: 20t;
Richard Levine/Alamy: 27t; Pavel Losevsky/Shutterstock: 16;
Luoman/istockphoto: 10: Robin Mackenzie/Shutterstock: 13b;
Manor Photography/Alamy: 20b; © Marine StewardshipCouncil:
19t; Karl Marttila/Alamy: 14tr; Monkey Business Images/
Shutterstock: 27b; Photospin Inc/Alamy: 14bl; Pot of Grass
Productions/Shutterstock: 7t; Paul Prescott/Alamy: 12; Viorika
Prikhodko/istockphoto: 6; Mark Ross/Shutterstock: 23b; Alex
Segre/Alamy: 22; US Stock Images/Alamy: 7b. Vegware
Ltd/vegware.co.uk: 23t; Peter Viisimaa/istockphoto: 9b; Joao
Vinissimo/Shutterstock: 18b; Alison Wright/Corbis: 11t. Sergey
Zavalnyuk/Alamy: 15.

To Rache for our inherited and shared love of cooking.

February 2011
RD/6000006415/001

"During 25 years of writing about the environment for the Guardian, I quickly realized that education was the first step to protecting the planet on which we all depend for survival. While the warning signs are everywhere that the Earth is heating up and the climate changing, many of us have been too preoccupied with living our lives to notice what is going on in our wider environment. It seems to me that it is children who need to know what is happening—they are often more observant of what is going on around them. We need to help them to grow up respecting and preserving the natural world on which their future depends. By teaching them about the importance of water, energy, and other key areas of life, we can be sure they will soon be influencing their parents' lifestyles, too. This is a series of books every child should read."

Paul Brown
Former environment correspondent for the UK's *Guardian* newspaper, environmental author, and fellow of Wolfson College, Cambridge, UK.

Contents

Where Does Our Food Come From?   6

The Cost of Food   8

The Price of Farming   10

Food Miles   12

What a Waste!   14

Waste Not, Want Not   16

The Choice is Yours   18

In Season!   20

Pack Light   22

Get a Bag Habit!   24

Power to the People!   26

Glossary   28

Useful Information   29

Index   30

Words in **bold** can be found in the glossary on page 28.

Where Does Our Food Come From?

What have you eaten today? A piece of fruit, a sandwich, or maybe a cookie or two? Have you ever really thought about where the food we eat comes from, how it gets to us, or what happens to any food that is left over?

Many kinds of fruit, including apples, are ready to eat as soon as they are ripe. No cooking or preparation is required!

Fresh Food

The food that we buy at the store comes from farms all over the world. Fruit, **cereal crops**, and vegetables are grown in fields, orchards, and greenhouses. Eggs and dairy products come from animals on farms, and meat comes from animals that have been specially bred for the purpose.

Processed Food

We eat some fresh foods, such as fruit and vegetables, in their **raw state**. But much of the food we buy today has been **processed** in some way. This means it has been changed from its raw state, for example, by cooking it, to make it into another food item or part of another food item, such as a box of cereal or a can of soup. Food processing takes place in factories.

Once food has been packaged, it may need refrigerating, too.

Packaging and Transporting

Once the food has been processed, it is packaged to make it easier to store and transport. It is also wrapped in plastic or foil to keep it fresh. It is then transported by road, sea, or air to the stores where it will be sold.

CASE STUDY

IN THE TRASH

In developed countries, we tend to take our food for granted, so much so that many of us waste a lot of food. On average, one out of every three grocery bags of food we buy is thrown away. That is not just packaging, but food that could actually still be eaten. In the U.S., one out of every four bags of groceries is thrown away.

Imagine putting one-third of all this food straight into the garbage.

The Cost of Food

You might think that the cost of your food is simply the money you hand over to buy it. But the real cost is much more complicated and expensive than that!

An Expensive Process

Growing our food, processing it, packaging it, storing some of it in refrigerators, and finally transporting it to the stores where it will be sold, all of these activities have another cost—a cost to our **environment**.

Fossil Fuels

Factories that process and wrap food products use electricity. Electricity is usually made by burning fuels such as coal, natural gas, or oil. Transporting food also uses fuel, usually gas or diesel. All of these fuels are known as **fossil fuels** because they were formed underground over millions of years from plant or animal remains. Earth's fossil fuels cannot be replaced and will eventually run out.

 The more a food is processed, the more energy is used.

Global Warming

Burning fossil fuels creates a gas called **carbon dioxide** (CO_2). Carbon dioxide is known as a **greenhouse gas** because it traps heat from the Sun inside the Earth's atmosphere, just like glass traps heat in a greenhouse. The atmosphere is the layer of air that surrounds the Earth. The extra CO_2 in the atmosphere is making the Earth heat up—this is called **global warming**.

Greenhouses trap the heat of the Sun to provide a warm place to grow plants.

Extreme weather has extreme results: this river has broken its banks.

Did you know?

Around 20 percent of greenhouse gases are related to the production, processing, transportation, and storage of food.

Climate Change

Earth's climate varies naturally, but evidence shows that people have made it change more quickly by burning more fossil fuels. As the temperature of the Earth changes, it changes our weather patterns. This is called **climate change**. Extreme weather events around the world, such as floods, droughts, and powerful storms, are becoming more common.

The Price of Farming

Farming gives us food and influences how we use and look after the countryside, but it can also cause problems for the environment.

Disappearing Forests

The world's **population** increases every year, so more food is needed. As a result, more forests around the world are being changed into farmland where farmers can grow crops and raise cattle. This is known as **deforestation**. The **rain forest** in countries such as Brazil is being cleared at a rate of 36 football fields a minute for farming and industry. Deforestation destroys the world's natural environment: it adds to global warming; removes animals' **habitats**; and can cause local flooding.

More and more areas of forest are being cut down to provide land to grow crops or pasture to graze animals.

Did you know?

When cattle digest grass, they produce a greenhouse gas called methane. Methane is more than 20 times more damaging than CO_2.

CASE STUDY

BREATHING TREES

Rain forests are precious for many reasons. They are the natural habitat of many species of insects and animals. They are a source of many natural ingredients for medicines. And trees use CO_2 to grow. This means they absorb, or take in, a lot of the CO_2 that we create through burning fossil fuels. But if we cut more and more trees down, we lose this natural way to balance our actions.

The rain forests can be harvested for vital ingredients to make medicines.

Fertilizers and Pesticides

Many farmers use chemicals such as **fertilizers** and **pesticides** on their crops. Fertilizers help crops to grow, and pesticides protect crops from insects and diseases. Both of these can be washed into local rivers, lakes, and ponds where they can kill wildlife and pollute drinking water. They also sink into the ground, where they build up over time and make the soil less **fertile**.

The pesticide spray from a tractor covers the soil as well as the crops. It can seep down into the ground and get into our groundwater.

Food Miles

Did you know that in order to reach your plate, your food could have traveled more than 1,250 miles (2,000 km)? Today, supermarkets sell food from all over the world. This means that we can choose from a variety of food all year round, but our food's journey also has a big environmental cost.

Transportation Toll

If the food you are eating has been grown locally, it might not have had far to travel, but nowadays food is often grown in a different country from where it is eaten. Transporting food from one country to another uses huge amounts of fuel and so creates a lot of CO_2.

 Some bananas eaten in the U.S. have traveled from South or Central America, or even the Caribbean.

Farm to Fork

Food miles try to measure how far our food has traveled from "farm to fork"—that is from the fields where it is grown to our plate. Food miles are based on how much CO_2 our food has made along its journey, including the fertilizer it took to grow it, the fuel it took to transport it, the energy it used to process and store it before you paid for it and took it home, and so on.

Grow Abroad

For some foods, in terms of food miles, it may be better to grow them abroad. In some colder countries, it is possible to grow tomatoes—even in wintertime—by planting them in greenhouses or polytunnels. But it takes a lot of fuel to heat a greenhouse or polytunnel in winter, so it can be more environmentally friendly to grow them in a warm country, and then transport them to a cold country.

Polytunnels are plastic shelters that can be used to grow a variety of foods, in particular soft fruits.

FOOD MILE FACTS

A recent U.S. study found out that the ingredients of strawberry yogurt—strawberries, milk, and sugar—had traveled more than 2,200 miles (3,540 km) before reaching the supermarket.

How far has your dessert traveled?

What a Waste!

Every day around the world, millions of tons of leftover food is thrown away. Throwing food away is not just a waste of money, it also pollutes our environment and contributes to the problem of global warming.

Wasting Away

Developed countries are the worst culprits when it comes to throwing away food. It is estimated that in the United States, 25 million tons of food are thrown away every year—that's enough to fill the Rose Bowl every three days. In the UK, 6.7 million tons of food is thrown away a year—this includes one million slices of ham, 1.3 million cartons of yogurt, and enough apples to fill 24 buses *a day*. Australians throw out three million tons of food a year. That's enough to feed the whole country for three weeks.

 Can you imagine this enormous stadium filled with unwanted food? What a waste.

Hidden Costs

This isn't just a waste of food, it's also a waste of the **natural resources** taken to grow the food. To grow the three million tons of food thrown away in Australia a year wastes enough water to fill Sydney Harbor three times! Throwing food away also wastes a lot of money. And simply dumping unwanted food in the trash can wastes space as well. In the U.S., nearly one-fifth of food waste ends up in **landfill**.

A lot of our waste, including food scraps, ends up being buried in the ground in landfill. Rotting food gives off the greenhouse gas methane.

A Source of Pollution

Throwing so much food away also contributes to the worldwide problem of global warming. For example, if the UK alone didn't waste the amount of food it does, it would save 18 million tons of CO_2 being released into the air each year. That's like taking one in five cars (whose exhaust fumes cause CO_2 pollution) off the roads.

WORRYING WASTE

In the United States, restaurants throw away more than 6,000 tons of food every day. In terms of weight, that's the same as 1,000 Asian male elephants.

Throwing away just 2 pounds (1 kg) of white rice wastes 525 gallons (2,385 l) of water that went into making it. That's enough water to fill nearly 30 bathtubs!

Waste Not, Want Not

By reducing our food waste, we can save ourselves money, make less pollution, and use less energy. There are many things we can do to reduce our food waste. You may do some of them already.

A Smart Plan!

To start with, you could help to plan a week's menu with your family. By planning meals in advance, you are more likely to buy only the food you need, and if you help choose what's on the menu, you're more likely to eat it, too!

 Get involved and help with the grocery shopping.

Sensible Shopping

Once you've planned a week's menu, try to write a shopping list and take it with you when you go. Help out in the supermarket by checking "best before" and "use-by" dates. Buy food items with the latest date, so you have more time to use your ingredients and you don't end up throwing them away because they have gone rotten or moldy.

Check the Cupboard

Keep basic ingredients such as canned tomatoes in the cupboard. Whoever does most of the cooking in your household will have their favorite ingredients and it is useful to have some basics that can be added to lots of different dishes. This will help use up leftovers and means you don't have to drive to the store for just one item.

 Basic foods, such as rice and pasta, are always useful to have in the cupboard.

Did you know?

The British store Marks & Spencer is researching using food waste to power its 500 stores across the UK.

When I asked you to make something with the leftovers, I meant something we could eat!

Portion Control!

Have you ever heard the expression "Your eyes were bigger than your stomach?" This is when you put more food on your plate than you can eat. Try to take only what you need and no more. Be sure to eat at least five portions of fruit and vegetables a day, though. But if you can't finish your meal, try turning your leftovers into creative dishes. There are lots of recipes you could try, so look on the Internet with your parent or carer for ideas.

The Choice is Yours

We make many choices about our food that make a difference to our environment, from what we choose to eat to how often we go to the supermarket.

 These cattle in Brazil are grazing on land that used to be rain forest.

Meat and Two Vegetables

Did you know that due to the demand for beef, there are about 1.3 billion cattle on Earth? These cattle take up about one-quarter of the land on the planet and they eat enough grain to feed millions of people. Raising this amount of cattle causes more CO_2 pollution than the pollution caused by transportation and uses up a lot of our water supply. We don't have to stop eating beef, but for the sake of our environment we should think about whether we need to eat as much beef as we do.

Did you know?

It is believed that every hamburger made from certain Central American beef results in the loss to the rain forest of, on average, one large tree, about 50 saplings, and 20–30 seedlings.

Shop With Care

Stores can only sell what people will buy. If we all choose to buy food that has been grown with care, or packaged responsibly, this is another way to help our environment. Some people choose to eat **organic foods**, which are usually grown using more natural methods, reducing the amount of chemicals used to make crops grow or to control pests. However, growing organic crops does take up more land than growing crops using chemicals.

 Look for the Marine Stewardship logo on fish and fish products.

Spot the Symbol

Look for the symbols or logos on packaging that show the food has been produced using methods that are environmentally friendly. For example, the Marine Stewardship logo shows that the item has been fished from **sustainable** stocks.

Food ordered online saves a trip to the grocery store.

Get Online

Did you know that in some countries, half of the distance clocked up in cars is from traveling to and from the supermarket? If stores in your area offer the service, try shopping online. Also, try to build up a list of things you need, rather than going to the supermarket to buy just one item.

In Season!

When your grandma or grandpa were children, less food was **imported** from other countries. This meant people mostly ate food that was grown locally and was **in season**. This was better for the environment. It meant that the food grew naturally at that time of year and needed less energy to make it grow.

Go Local

Food that is grown in season and sold locally can be fresher, and often tastier, because it hasn't had to travel far or be stored for long. Many supermarkets now offer locally grown produce so you can choose foods that have taken less energy to grow, and clocked up fewer food miles along the way.

 Farmer's markets sell fresh, locally grown food such as fruit, vegetables, eggs, and cheese.

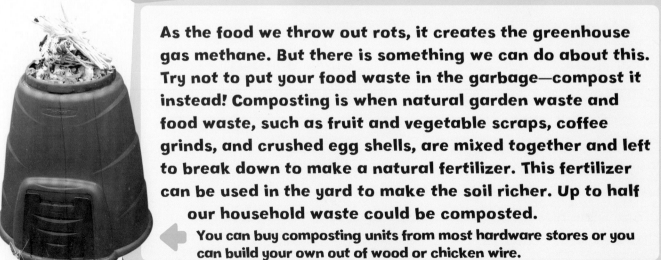

CASE STUDY

COMPOSTING

As the food we throw out rots, it creates the greenhouse gas methane. But there is something we can do about this. Try not to put your food waste in the garbage—compost it instead! Composting is when natural garden waste and food waste, such as fruit and vegetable scraps, coffee grinds, and crushed egg shells, are mixed together and left to break down to make a natural fertilizer. This fertilizer can be used in the yard to make the soil richer. Up to half our household waste could be composted.

You can buy composting units from most hardware stores or you can build your own out of wood or chicken wire.

Grow Your Own

Why not try growing your own fruit and vegetables? You can't get much fresher than that! If you live in an apartment, you and your family can still grow vegetables on a balcony or you could join or start a gardening club at school.

 Growing your own food can be fun, as well as giving you fresh fruit and vegetables to eat.

When I said natural things could go in the compost, I didn't mean your brother!

WHAT A LOAD OF GARBAGE!

In Victoria in Australia, nearly half of waste sent to landfill is green or food waste, much of which could be composted.

Pack Light

Today, more than half of all packaging is used to package food. But it is possible to help reduce the amount of packaging that ends up in landfill from our food products.

Less Is More

When you go shopping, try to buy food items with less packaging. Try not to buy things that are individually wrapped, such as cookies in separate wrappers, for example. Also, where possible, choose to buy food in packaging that can be **recycled**, or better still, buy food that's in recycled packaging that can be recycled!

These bananas don't need their plastic packaging—they have their skins to protect them!

PACKAGING

Some retailers are trying to make their packaging greener. Research has been done into finding a material that will rot or break down and so not take up space in landfill.

The British retailers Marks & Spencer have already produced and sold more than 132 million sandwiches packed in corn-based plastic packaging.

This sandwich packaging is made from corn so it can be composted.

Food Packaging

To help decide what to do with any food packaging, look for labels on the packaging that can help you. If your sandwich has come in a corn-based package, it may have a composting symbol on it so you know you can compost it safely. Plastics and glass often have the recycling triangle; where a number appears in the middle, this tells you how to group your plastics. The mobius loop is a well-known recycling symbol.

Did you know?

In 2006, 43,000 tons of green packaging was used worldwide—that's about the same weight as 6,000 fully grown African elephants!

The mobius loop is used around the world to show that something can be recycled.

Get a Bag Habit!

Does your family take your own bags with you when you go shopping? If you don't, now is the time to get a "bag habit"! Plastic bags are one of the biggest sources of pollution in the world and most of the time, they are used once and then thrown away.

"Take an old bag shopping"

People are becoming more concerned about the effect that throwing away billions of plastic shopping bags is having on our environment. "Get a bag habit" or "take an old bag shopping" are a couple of the campaigns used by governments and supermarkets to encourage us to remember to take reusable bags with us when we buy our groceries.

We may only use a plastic bag for a few minutes, but it can take 500 years for the bag to break down. And before it does, it can litter our countryside and endanger wildlife.

Did you know?
It is claimed that 8.7 plastic shopping bags contain enough petroleum energy in them to drive a car for half a mile (1 km).

BAGS GALORE

Americans use more than 380 billion polyethylene bags every year and throw away approximately 100 billion of them. The bags are carried by wind into forests, ponds, rivers, and lakes where wildlife can mistake them for food. Some figures suggest that one billion seabirds and 100,000 marine mammals die from eating plastic bags every year.

Taxing Bags

Some retailers are doing their best to help solve the problem of people not reusing their plastic bags. In recent years, many grocers and retailers have introduced plastic bag collection programs, offering centers where you can recycle your plastic bags.

Some retailers, such as this British one, allow customers to recycle their plastic bags.

CARRIER BAGS ONLY

Carrier bag RECYCLING

New Products

Recycled plastic bags can be turned into new, and sometimes surprising, products. If you're handy with a knitting needle, plastic bags can be made into new knitted reusable bags, blankets, and rugs. Some artists have even turned plastic bags into works of art to draw attention to the problem of plastic-bag waste.

Artists have created these chicken ornaments out of plastic bags.

Power to the People!

Have you heard of the three Rs—reduce, reuse, and recycle? Well, we can do that with food waste as well as general waste. We can reduce the amount we buy and eat, reuse our leftovers, and recycle food packaging or any food waste by composting it. If we all act together, we can make a big difference.

Less Is Best!

You can tell when Christmas is over because Easter candy starts to appear in the stores! If you celebrate Easter, you will probably look forward to getting chocolate eggs or a bunny. But how many times have you opened a chocolate Easter treat to find that it was mostly packaging?

Customers started to complain, so companies who make chocolate Easter eggs, such as Nestlé and Cadbury's, have reduced their packaging. As a result, in 2009, the cuts Nestlé made in the UK alone saved 700 tons of waste. There was less packaging, so more eggs could fit in the trucks, too, which saved 48,000 miles (77,249 km) of road transportation and reduced the amount of CO_2 given off.

Companies do listen to public concern and have recently cut down on wasteful packaging.

MAKING USE OF FOOD WASTE

In New York City, a charity called City Harvest collects food waste from restaurants, stores, factories, and so on, and takes it to homeless shelters, soup kitchens, and care centers to feed the hungry and homeless. In an average year, they collect 23 million lb. (10.4 million kg) of food. In December 2008, New York schoolchildren added 60,000 lb. (27,215 kg) of food to this—that's heavier than 100 black bears!

Volunteers help package apples for the homeless in a City Harvest project in Union Square, New York.

A Wise Choice

People power really can work. Use it wisely to try to encourage retailers to sell food that has been grown in an environmentally friendly way, packaged only when necessary, and with green packaging that can be composted. Use your own power wisely to make careful choices about what food you choose to eat and buy.

Remember to look at the labels before you buy your food to see if it has been grown in an environmentally friendly way.

Glossary

Carbon dioxide A gas in the air around us.

Cereal crops Crops that are grown to produce grain, such as wheat.

Climate change Long-term changes to the world's weather patterns.

Deforestation The cutting down of large areas of forests by people.

Developed countries Countries that are wealthy and rely on money from industry; and where most people work in factories and businesses rather than in farming.

Energy The power to make or do something.

Environment Surroundings.

Fertile In this instance, land that can produce healthy crops.

Fertilizer A substance, either natural or chemical, that is given to plants or put on the soil to make plants grow well.

Fossil fuels Fuels, such as coal, oil, or gas, that have developed under the ground from rotting animal and plant life over millions of years.

Global warming The gradual heating up of the Earth's atmosphere.

Greenhouse gas A gas, such as carbon dioxide, that creates an invisible layer around the Earth, keeping in the heat of the Sun's rays.

Groundwater Water that is held underground in rocks and soil.

Habitat The natural surroundings in which an animal or plant usually lives.

Imported When products or goods are brought in from one country to another.

In season In this instance, when a food is available during its natural growing time.

Landfill Areas for dumping and burying household or industrial waste.

Natural resources Materials, such as water and wood, that are found in nature.

Organic foods Foods that have been grown using natural methods, without relying on chemical fertilizers or pesticides.

Pesticides Chemicals used to kill unwanted pests and diseases on plants.

Population The number of people living in a place.

Processed In this instance, to do with adding chemicals to food in order to preserve, or keep it fresh, for longer.

Rain forest A forest in an area that usually receives a lot of rain.

Raw state In this instance, a food that hasn't been processed, or chemically changed in any way, but is eaten in the form in which it has grown.

Recycle To break something down so the materials it is made of can be used again.

Sustainable Able to be used now and in the future.

Useful Information

Throughout this book, "real-life measurements" are used for reference. These measurements are not exact, but give a sense of just how much an amount is, or what it looks like.

1 full bathtub = 21 GALLONS (80 L)

American black bear = 595 LB. (270 KG)

Asian elephant = 5 TONS

African elephant = 7 TONS

Olympic-size pool = 660,430 GALLONS (2,500,000 L)

Further reading

Food and Farming (Sustainable World) by Rob Bowden (Wayland, 2007)

Green Team: Your Food by Sally Hewitt (Crabtree Publishing Company, 2008)

Going Green: Eating Green by Sunita Apte (Bearport Publishing, 2009)

Web Sites

www.lovefoodhatewaste.com
Recipes, food-saving tips, and how to avoid waste.

www.greenchoices.org/index.php?page=food
All about the choices we make about what we eat.

www.kidsgardening.org/
A site to encourage children to make good food choices and build a love of nature through gardening.

Dates to Remember

Earth Hour—March 28

Earth Day—April 22

World Environment Day—June 5

Clean Air Day—June

Walk to School Campaign—May and October

World Food Day—October 16

America Recycles Day—November 15

Note to parents and teachers: Every effort has been made by the Publishers to ensure that these web sites are suitable for children, that they are of the highest educational value, and that they contain no inappropriate or offensive material. However, because of the nature of the Internet, it is impossible to guarantee that the contents of these sites will not be altered. We strongly advise that Internet access is supervised by a responsible adult

Index

atmosphere 9, 28
Australia 7, 14, 15, 21

Brazil 10, 18

carbon dioxide 9, 10, 11, 12, 15, 18, 26, 28
climate change 9, 28
composting 20, 21, 23, 26, 27

deforestation 10, 28
developed countries 7, 14, 28

energy 8, 12, 16, 20, 24, 28

farm animals 6, 10, 18
farming 6, 10–11, 12, 15, 19, 27, 28
fertilizers 11, 12, 20, 28
food miles 12–13, 20
food processing 7, 8, 9, 12, 28
food storage 7, 8, 9, 12, 20
food waste 7, 14–15, 16, 17, 20, 21, 26, 27
fossil fuels 8, 9, 11, 12, 13, 28

global warming 9, 10, 14, 15, 28
greenhouse gases 9, 10, 15, 20, 28
groundwater 11, 28
grow your own 21

habitats 10, 11, 28

landfill 15, 21, 22, 23, 28

local food 12, 20

Marine Stewardship 19
Marks & Spencer 17, 23
methane 10, 15, 20

natural resources 15, 28

organic farming 19, 28

packaging 7, 8, 19, 22–23, 26, 27
pesticides 11, 28
plastic bags 24–25
pollution 11, 14, 15, 16, 18, 24
population 10, 28

rain forests 10, 11, 18, 28
recycle 22, 23, 25, 26

saving money 16
seasonal foods 20–21, 28
shopping 6, 16, 17, 18, 19, 22, 24, 25
supermarkets 7, 12, 13, 16, 19, 20, 23, 24, 25, 27

transportation 7, 8, 9, 12, 13, 17, 18, 19, 20, 26

UK 14, 15, 17, 23, 26
United States 7, 13, 14, 15, 27

water supply 15, 18